MIA MAYHEM

BREAKS DOWN WALLS

CRASH!

BY **KARA WEST**   ILLUSTRATED BY **LEEZA HERNANDEZ**

LITTLE SIMON

New York   London   Toronto   Sydney   New Delhi

LITTLE SIMON

An imprint of Simon & Schuster Children's Publishing Division
1230 Avenue of the Americas, New York, New York 10020
First Little Simon paperback edition July 2019
Copyright © 2019 by Simon & Schuster, Inc.
Also available in a Little Simon hardcover edition
All rights reserved, including the right of reproduction in whole or in part in any form.
LITTLE SIMON is a registered trademark of Simon & Schuster, Inc., and associated colophon is a trademark of Simon & Schuster, Inc.
For information about special discounts for bulk purchases, please contact Simon & Schuster Special Sales at 1-866-506-1949 or business@simonandschuster.com.
The Simon & Schuster Speakers Bureau can bring authors to your live event. For more information or to book an event contact the Simon & Schuster Speakers Bureau at 1-866-248-3049 or visit our website at www.simonspeakers.com.
Designed by Laura Roode
Manufactured in the United States of America 0619 MTN
2 4 6 8 10 9 7 5 3 1
Library of Congress Cataloging-in-Publication Data
Names: West, Kara, author. | Hernandez, Leeza, illustrator.
Title: Mia mayhem breaks down walls / by Kara West ; illustrated by Leeza Hernandez.
Description: First Little Simon paperback edition. | New York : Little Simon, 2019. | Series: Mia mayhem ; 4 | Summary: Unable to control her superstrength, Mia accidentally causes mayhem at school and must rely on her friends to help her repair things.
Identifiers: LCCN 2019011417 | ISBN 9781534444768 (paperback) | ISBN 9781534444775 (hardcover) | ISBN 9781534444782 (eBook)
Subjects: | CYAC: Ability—Fiction. | Self-control—Fiction. | Superheroes—Fiction. | Friendship—Fiction. | Schools—Fiction. | African Americans—Fiction. | BISAC: JUVENILE FICTION / Action & Adventure / General. | JUVENILE FICTION / Readers / Chapter Books.
Classification: LCC PZ7.1.W43684 Mf 2019 | DDC [E]—dc23
LC record available at https://lccn.loc.gov/2019011417

CONTENTS

THE GOOD LUCK CHARM

My room is a mess. I'm digging around in my closet because I've ripped another shoelace.

This is the fifth one I've ripped in two days. The *fifth*! For some reason, they keep tearing in half when I try to pull the bunny ears through the loop.

Don't ask me why. The only answer I've got is this: Disasters, even tiny

little shoelace-size disasters, follow me around everywhere.

They happen during the day at regular school. And they also happen *after* school, at the Program for In Training Superheroes, aka the PITS. That's the top secret training academy where I learn how to use my superpowers!

Yeah, you heard me right.

My name is Mia Macarooney, and *I. Am. A. Superhero!*

But at the PITS, I go by Mia Mayhem.

And guess what? So far, I've learned how to fly *and* run with superspeed.

But here's the thing: Even superheroes sometimes have shoelace trouble.

So that's why there was a huge mess on my floor when my mom walked into my room.

"Hey, sweetie. There's something I want to give you," she said as she sat down.

"Is it a new shoelace?" I asked.

"No, it's *way* better than a shoelace," she replied.

Then she held out a small box.

I took it from her hand and opened it. Inside, on top of a tiny cushion, was a shiny star pendant with a single blue stone in the middle, and lightning bolts on either side. It was the coolest necklace I'd ever seen.

"Wow, this is *so* cool!" I cried. "Is it my birthday today?"

"Ha! No, it isn't," she said, smiling. "But I know how hard you've been working lately. Going to regular school *and* juggling PITS training is a lot."

I nodded. It *was* a lot sometimes.

"Your grandma gave this to me after *I* started training at the PITS. This was her necklace when *she* was a girl, and I think you're ready to have it. It's a family good luck charm!"

Good luck charm? Perfect. I needed all the luck I could get right now.

I thanked my mom and gave her a huge hug before she left.

Then I took a better look at the necklace. It was the perfect shade of blue and would even go with my suit.

It was so pretty that I couldn't stop staring at it.

9

But then I had to. Because my cat suddenly jumped up, pushed me down, and started licking me like crazy before running off.

"Oh, Chaos! I can't play right now!"
I told her, sitting back up.

I love my cat, but sometimes she is
a handful. Even for me.

I opened my hands to put the necklace on.

But then my stomach dropped.

My hands were empty.

I got up and did a quick scan of the floor. Then I checked all my pockets, took off my socks, and even looked inside my dirty old shoe.

But the necklace was gone!

CHAPTER 2

THE CAT-TASTROPHE

I'd been distracted for only *one minute.*
That's it. *One minute!*

But somehow, a tiny shoelace
disaster had become an epic missing
necklace search.

"Hey, Chaos!" I yelled, totally
panicked. "Where is my necklace?"

I got down on my knees and looked
at her face-to-face.

"You hid the necklace, didn't you? Just so I'd play?"

She gave no response. But trust me. I know a cat smirk when I see one.

And the necklace *had* to be somewhere in my room. I just needed to know where to look.

I threw my favorite cat pillow off my bed.

Nope, not there.

So I picked up the bed itself and peeked under.

Lots of dust bunnies, but nope . . . not there either.

So next, I dumped all the dirty clothes out of my hamper.

Lots of smelly clothes, but again, no necklace.

Right then, as if on cue, Chaos dragged a pair of dirty pants across the floor, while wearing one of my socks!

Now usually, I'd run around chasing her . . . and make an even bigger mess.

But today, I really didn't have time. So I stayed focused and kept searching.

I lifted up my dresser with one hand and checked under there.

Then I tossed it next to my dirty clothes.

Then I threw my chair on top.

Then my desk.

Then my bookcase, too.

Before I knew it, everything was stacked on top of one another.

But I still had *no* necklace.

Oh boy.

What was I supposed to tell my mom?

I looked up and saw Chaos lying on top of the bookcase near the ceiling. And that's when I remembered: I'd been too busy looking *under* my stuff that I forgot that Chaos actually loves climbing to the very top of things . . . even if she can't get back down.

My parents don't usually use their powers inside the house.

So I'm guessing I shouldn't either. But *this* was an emergency.

I flew to the top of the bookcase and grabbed Chaos with both hands.

And that's when I saw it: The shiny star necklace was around her neck, hanging right in front of me this whole time.

Now, don't ask me how she got the necklace on. I have no idea. But it doesn't matter. I finally found it!

When we were back on the floor, I took the necklace from Chaos. Then I put it back inside the tiny jewelry box. After all that mayhem, I definitely was *not* going to wear it today.

I tucked the box safely underneath my blanket and then looked around. My room was a total disaster.

Hopefully, my mom wouldn't notice because this mess would have to wait.

Right now, it was time for Power Hour at the PITS!

THE POWER HOUR

You know what's awesome about having superspeed? It really comes in handy when I'm late for my PITS training.

See what I mean? I'm already here! With even a few minutes to spare.

I did my quick superhero change trick and turned the DO NOT ENTER sign. A hidden screen popped up and scanned my face.

Pretty cool, right?

Well, let me tell you. It's even *cooler* on the inside. From the outside, no one would ever guess that this building is a top secret training academy for superheroes . . . just like me!

The front entrance slid open, and I walked in. The main lobby, also known as the Compass, was really crowded today. Luckily, I was able to squeeze into the elevator going to the second level. That was where all the junior level classes were held.

Once I hopped off the elevator, I found Professor Dina Myte's classroom.

When I walked in, my jaw dropped to the floor. There was a full-size airplane right in front of me! But that wasn't all. Next to it, there was a big rig with seven cars, a cruise ship, a submarine, a tractor, random telephone poles, and even a Ferris wheel.

"I hope we get to ride that," whispered a friendly voice.

I turned around. It was Allie Oomph!

"Yeah, that'd be AWESOME!" I agreed.

I gave Allie a huge hug just as Penn Powers walked over.

"Hey, guys!" Penn said. "Ready for the Power Hour?"

We both nodded excitedly.

When Penn and I first met, we didn't exactly get along. But luckily, that changed after he helped me in flying class. And then came Allie. Penn and I met her in superspeed class, and we became friends in a flash.

The bell rang just as Professor Myte appeared. "Welcome to your first Power Hour, everyone!" she said warmly.

I smiled at Penn and Allie.

"I hope you're all excited. We're going to start the lesson with some special guests. Please give them a warm welcome!" Professor Myte cheered.

Then, right on cue, a giant potbellied pig, three hippos, two camels, and an elephant walked in.

Now, believe it or not, I've already lifted an elephant before. It was part of my PITS placement exam. But I have no idea how I did it last time. Honestly, I think I was just lucky. So I kind of wish I *had* brought my new good luck charm. But it was too late to worry now.

"All right, class," Professor Myte continued. "There's only one very important rule to controlling your strength: Keep your feet grounded and focus your energy in one place. Focus is key. Without it, this superpower can be very dangerous. But if you lift correctly, even the heaviest objects will be as light as a feather."

Everyone then broke up into groups of three. And Allie, Penn, and I got to work.

Penn walked over, bent down, and easily picked up one of the camels.

Just like that!

Then Allie did the same . . . but with double the weight!

One camel was impressive. But one in each arm? That was crazy.

I wasn't sure I could follow her.

But luckily, Professor Myte was right! The hippo really was as light as a feather.

After that, unlike some of the other kids in class, we breezed through everything.

From the cars,

to the cruise ship,

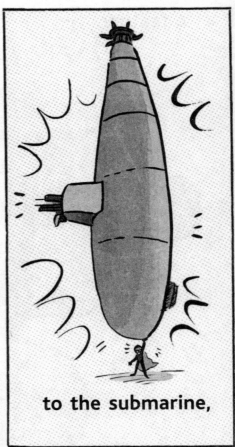

to the submarine,

and even to the tractor.

At this rate, maybe I didn't even need a good luck charm?

CRASH!

Or maybe I did.

CHAPTER 4

How Strong Is Too Strong?

So, the next morning, I wore my new good luck charm around my neck. Then I walked to regular school, with my best friend, Eddie, just like always.

Now, Eddie's my only friend who knows my super-secret. I admit, sometimes I wish I could tell the whole world. But as a superhero, I need to protect my secret identity.

I'm *so* glad I don't have to keep it from Eddie, though.

Having someone on my side is really nice. Because when you're just discovering that you have superpowers, weird things can happen.

Like pulling off a doorknob by mistake.

I looked at Eddie. And Eddie looked at me.

"Oh, how weird!" Eddie said so everybody could hear. "What a flimsy old doorknob!"

I gave Eddie a knowing shrug and handed the loose knob to my teacher.

At my desk, I plopped my backpack down like I always did.

But then one of the desk legs snapped right in two!

Luckily, my teacher moved me to an empty desk . . . without asking any questions. Sitting in the back, I hoped that I was in the clear for a normal-ish day. Until I broke *every single one* of my pencils.

PLOP!

SNAP!

I had no idea what was going on, but I *needed* to take a break.

In the bathroom, I splashed some water on my face and looked at the shiny blue necklace in the mirror. It *looked* awesome, but so far, it was *not* bringing me any luck.

I leaned over to turn off the water. When I touched the faucet, the whole thing snapped off! Spraying water EVERYWHERE!

I backed away from the sink and bumped into the stalls behind me.

Now, I really didn't hit them that hard. But the next thing I knew, there was a loud creaking sound . . . and then the entire row of stalls toppled over! Within seconds, I was standing in the middle of a giant bathroom disaster.

SPACE

Uh-oh. I had no idea what was happening. But I knew I *had* to leave before I made things worse.

Out in the hall, Mrs. Cruz, the principal, was passing by.

"Um, excuse me," I said with a shaky voice. "There's . . . a plumbing problem in that bathroom."

Oh boy. I know I have a bit of a reputation for causing mayhem. But this has got to be one of my worse disasters *ever*.

CHAPTER 5

EDDIE'S SUPERPOWER

As I walked back into class, I took a deep breath and tried to look as normal as possible. I wanted to tell Eddie what happened. But with everyone around, it would have to wait.

For the rest of the morning, I moved as little as possible to keep from causing more mayhem.

But when it was time for gym class,

I knew it'd be a *very* bad idea for me to play volleyball. That is, unless I wanted to punch a hole in the gym ceiling.

So I stood in the very back and didn't dare to touch anything.

"Hey, Mia! What's going on?" Eddie asked during a break. "You usually love volleyball."

Before I opened my mouth, I made sure nobody was near us.

Then I took a deep breath and let it all out.

"My superpowers are out of whack. I keep breaking every single thing I touch!"

"Hmm, is this related to that time you broke the soccer goalposts by mistake?" Eddie asked.

"Yes, but that happened *before* I knew I was a superhero. Things are different this time," I explained. "I would never try to use my powers here. But earlier this morning, I broke everything in the girls' bathroom . . . by mistake!"

"No way! How bad do things look?" he asked.

"Really bad. That bathroom is going to be out of order for a *long* time," I replied.

Eddie scrunched up his face. I could tell he was thinking hard.

"Hey, remember the nifty helper bot I built?" he finally asked after a long pause.

Of course I did. Eddie was the smartest person I knew. And he loved building and designing robots.

"Yeah, that robot was supposed to be a cleaning helper, but it nearly destroyed your house!" I replied.

He nodded and let out a small laugh.

"I know you're feeling unlucky. And I have to admit, mayhem really *does* follow you around. But I've had my own trouble too . . . and I'm not even *super*!" he said. "Things might be crazy now, but trust me. Everything will be okay."

"You think so?" I asked quietly.

"Totally," he said. "I know how hard learning to fly was. But I believed in you. With practice, you figured out how to fly! We even tracked all those puppies together, remember?"

I was still really embarrassed. But I knew he was right.

Because like Eddie just said, he might not be literally *super* like me . . . but as we did our secret handshake, I realized that if he *did* have powers, it'd be that he could be a *super*-awesome friend.

CHAPTER
6

THE CRASH CLASS

I arrived at the PITS in a much better mood thanks to Eddie's pep talk. Allie and Penn were already there. When I sat down, Penn noticed that there was something different about my suit.

"Hey, Mia! Cool necklace!" he said.

"Oh, thanks!" I said proudly. "It was my mother's. And my grandmother's before her. It's a good luck charm!"

"How neat!" Allie exclaimed. "I wish I had a good luck charm too."

I nodded. It was certainly nice to have.

But as far as physical strength goes, Allie didn't need any luck.

I mean, come on. Did you see her lifting those camels? If anyone needed luck, it was *me*.

Right then, our teacher came bursting through the doors.

"All right, class. Yesterday we found out how strong you all are," she began. "But today is the real test—when you'll learn how to *control* your strength."

My ears perked up. This was *definitely* something I needed to learn.

We got into the same groups as yesterday. Then Professor Myte explained the rules.

"You'll need to lift and move the vehicle in front of you to the other side of the room. But here's the catch: The floor of every parking spot is covered in glass. So you must put each car down very gently."

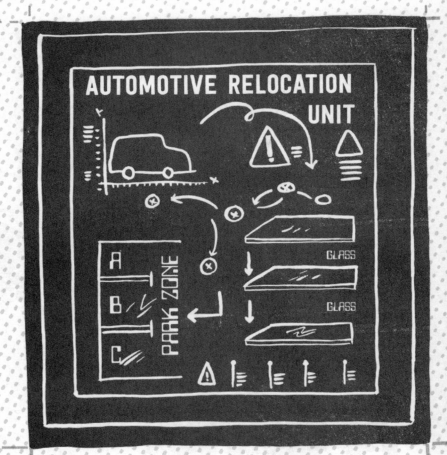

Oh boy. I was totally not ready for this. Lucky for me, there were no rules on how fast or slow we had to move.

So Penn tried to fly.

Allie decided to run.

And me?

I walked. Really slowly.

And at first, I wasn't that bad!

I easily lifted my car up into the air. I was about halfway across the room when my hands started to get really sweaty. And then I lost my grip.

A headlight and windshield wiper went flying off. And I dropped the car two more times before I even got to the glass floor. Now I just needed to figure out how to let go of the car without dropping it.

I looked over at Allie. She was already on her second round! I watched as she gently placed her car in the spot.

Wow. I didn't know how much practice it was going to take for me to match her level of control. But it was *not* going to happen today.

Just when I thought my luck couldn't get any worse . . . it did.

By the end of class, my car was in really bad shape. It was missing a door,

had no tires, and had a broken steering wheel.

As I stacked the flat tires in my arms, Hugo Fast, the class bully, pushed past me.

"Well, I guess not everyone's a natural," he said with a snicker as he walked away.

CHAPTER 7

THE SAVE-THE-DAY DISASTER

After class was over, Allie, Penn, and I headed to our lockers.

"Don't listen to Hugo, Mia," Allie said. "You'll get the hang of things."

"Yeah, Mia," Penn agreed. "Today was only the second class. I'm sure you'll have more luck tomorrow."

Penn had a huge smile. But then it went away.

"Oh no," he said in a quiet voice.

"Oh no, what?" I asked.

"Your good luck charm . . . is missing!"

I immediately touched my neck. He was right. It was gone!

I couldn't believe it. Did I really lose it *again*?

Without thinking, I rushed back to the classroom as fast as I could, with Penn and Allie right behind me.

When we got there, everything was exactly as we had left it.

A complete mess.

There were piles of loose bumpers, headlights, and windshield wipers everywhere. I took a deep breath and scanned the room.

This necklace search was going to

be *way* harder than digging through my closet. But thankfully, I had Penn and Allie. We decided to split up to cover the most ground.

I ran over to my run-down car. I leaned in and checked the front and back seats. There were lots of loose car parts, but no necklace.

So I moved on to the next car.

Then the next.

And the next.

As I moved down the line, I stacked each car on top of one another, just like I had done with my furniture.

The necklace had to be here

somewhere. But none of us was having any luck.

"I don't get it!" I finally cried. "It couldn't have walked out of here by itself, right?"

"Well, maybe it fell off after class, on our way to our lockers?" Allie suggested.

Oh no! The hallway?

If it was out there, who knew where it could be in this *huge* building?

I took a deep breath and tried to stay calm.

But that didn't work too well. Because I ran into a random classroom in a panic.

It was packed with a bunch of students who were doing Save-the-Day rescue exercises. According to Penn, Save-the-Day exercises were used to test a student's ability to think fast on their feet.

There were all sorts of awesome, but dangerous, rescue setups.

There was one kid stuck on a bridge.

UP HERE!

Another one
was on a water
tower.

And another one
was on a train!

BEEP!

BEEP!

Usually, I would totally be up for a rescue mission. But today I had my own job to complete.

As I rushed past the tall water tower, I instantly knew I was in trouble.

My jaw dropped to the floor as everything came falling down.

Oh no. I think I might have just destroyed the PITS!

CHAPTER 8

CODE MAROON

"Oh, Mia. What happened?" Dr. Sue Perb
asked when she walked in.

Dr. Sue Perb was the headmistress
of the PITS. She was the first superhero
(other than my parents) that I met.

I really wanted to go and hide. I just
searched my entire classroom, ruined
another, and still didn't have my family
necklace.

But I had a feeling Dr. Sue Perb would know what to do.

I took a deep breath and told her the truth.

"My mom gave me a necklace that is really special. *Her* mother gave it to *her*, and she gave it to me. But then I lost it. I've been looking for it everywhere, and I might have gotten carried away."

Dr. Perb raised an eyebrow.

"I didn't mean to. Really! I'm sorry," I began, looking up at her.

I was ready to be in trouble. I would be mad if I was her.

But instead, she patted me on the back and said, "I understand. A missing family necklace is, indeed, a serious situation."

After I explained what it looked like,
she pushed a few buttons on her watch
and spoke into it.

"Attention, students—Code Maroon.
I repeat, Code Maroon. We are opening
a school-wide search for Mia Mayhem's
missing star necklace." Dr. Sue Perb's
voice echoed through the hallways.

"Don't worry, Mia. We'll find it,"
Dr. Perb said. "It has to be *some*where."

"Oh, thank you SO much!" I cried.

I couldn't believe that all these busy
superheroes were going to look for my
necklace. At this rate, I was sure it
would pop up soon.

Penn, Allie, and I decided to retrace

my steps one more time. When we got back to Professor Myte's classroom, I was about to open the door, but Penn stopped me.

"Wait," he said. "You know, we weren't actually *in class* when we discovered it was missing."

"Oh yeah, that's right! We were at our lockers!" said Allie.

I was pretty sure I hadn't taken my necklace off. But at this point, it was worth looking again.

Back at my locker, I took everything out.

I had a random dirty shoe, Chaos's mouse toy, and even one of Eddie's  old robots. I had everything you could think of . . . except for the one thing I needed.

I was about to close the door when something caught my eye.

"Wait! I just saw a weird glow in the mirror!" I cried.

I flipped over my cape and touched around my neck.

I couldn't believe it. My star necklace was hidden against my suit all this time!

"Oh thank goodness! We found it!"
Allie cried.

Then the three of us ran to Dr. Sue
Perb's office to tell the school the good
news.

THE BIG PITS CLEAN

Dr. Perb called off the school-wide search as soon as we burst through her office door.

"Attention, students: The Code Maroon search has been solved. I repeat—the necklace has been found," Dr. Perb announced through her watch.

Once everything quieted down, I thanked her again.

It meant a lot to me that Dr. Perb, Allie, Penn, *and* the whole school cared about helping me find my family necklace.

"I'm so, so happy to have my necklace with me," I began. "But I feel a bit silly about the mess I created."

"Oh, Mia, I am very glad we've located the missing necklace. But may this be a good lesson for you."

I nodded as she patted my back.

Here's what I've learned after the craziest day: When I'm panicked, I really need to learn how to breathe and stay focused.

"But as superheroes, it's also important to help one another in times of need," Dr. Perb continued. "You needed help looking for the necklace, and now you'll need help cleaning up."

Oh boy. She was right. There was a *lot* to fix.

I wished I could put everything back together on my own. But there were so many things I didn't know how to do.

OOPS!

Like how to fix broken glass.

Or a water leak.

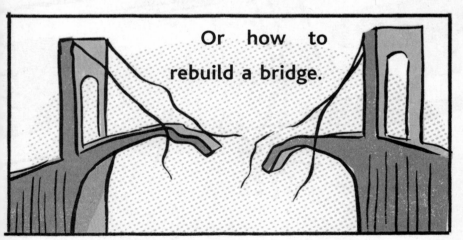

Or how to rebuild a bridge.

So Dr. Perb sent out another message to the entire school for volunteers.

Then she and Professor Myte split up the clean-up tasks in each room.

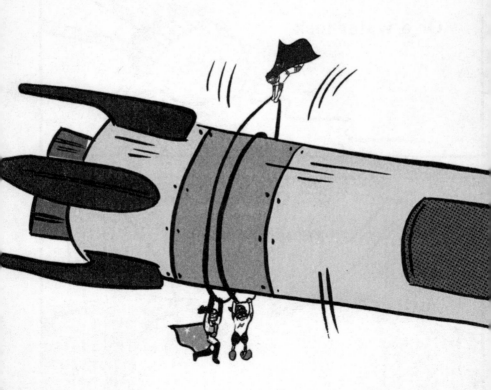

Bzzz!

Bzzz!

Some kids lifted heavy things (like
me, Allie, Penn, and even *Hugo*) while
other kids glued broken glass back
together . . .

restored metal,

and stacked
cement
bricks!

Pretty cool, right?

Clearly there are so many powers I still need to learn. But for now, I'm pretty happy about the fact that I can lift this car and put it back down in one piece. Without breaking anything else.

It turns out that Allie, Penn, and Eddie were right: All I needed was a bit of practice to figure out the perfect balance.

CHAPTER
10

ONE LAST THING

When I got home, I was so ready to flop right onto my bed and relax.

But I couldn't because I left my room looking like this!

My whole room was still a massive disaster. And of course, Chaos was curled up on my bed, taking a nap, as if she had nothing at all to do with the mess.

The good news is that I don't think my parents noticed. If they did, I definitely would have heard about it.

The cleanup at the PITS was a job for many, but I knew I could handle this mess on my own.

I easily moved my dresser, chair, and bed back into place.

Then I gathered all my dirty clothes and put them in the hamper.

I was just finishing up when there was a knock on my door.

"Come in!" I said.

Mom walked in and looked around my room.

I held my breath. Maybe she *did* know about the huge mess!

But then she just said, "Wow, Mia. Nice work. Your room looks great!"

I grinned widely and snuck Chaos a little wink.

"You're wearing the necklace! It looks terrific on you."

"Thanks, Mom. I love it!" I said.

Then she sat down on the bed next to me.

"You know, I remember the exact day your grandma gave it to me. But here's a little secret between you and me: I loved it too . . . but I lost it all the time!"

"What? No way!" I cried.

"Oh yeah!" my mom replied. "One time I broke the girls' bathroom and even broke an entire obstacle course at the PITS because I thought I lost it!"

My jaw dropped to the floor. I couldn't believe it.

That sounded way too similar to the day I just had. I knew that our superpowers ran in the family. But I didn't know that my mom was known for causing trouble like me. Does that mean it also runs in the family?

Whatever the case, if there's anything that today has taught me, it's that practice makes perfect.

I know I'll need some help along the way, but there are plenty of things I can now do on my own. Like fly, run, and lift things ten times my weight!

And when I need just a little bit of luck, I'll take out and wear my beautiful blue necklace.

But for the sake of avoiding another bathroom disaster story, I think it'd be best to keep this necklace tucked away for now. I have a funny feeling I'll know exactly when I really need it.

DON'T MISS
MIA MAYHEM'S
NEXT ADVENTURE!

"Mia Macarooney, why are you late again?" asked Mrs. Cruz.

That was a very good question.

I was standing in her office as she wrote me another tardy slip. She was the principal of Normal Elementary School.

Excerpt from *Mia Mayhem Stops Time!*

"Mia, this is the fourth time this week," she continued.

"I'm sorry. I'll try to make sure it won't happen again," I replied.

Mrs. Cruz paused, waiting for me to say more.

But I couldn't make any hard promises.

Because every day this week, something weird has happened to make me late. And I couldn't tell her why.

Why not, you ask?

Well, because . . . I've been using my superpowers!

Yeah, you heard me right.

My name is Mia, and I. AM. A. SUPERHERO!

Right now, during regular school, I'm Mia Macarooney.

But when the school bell rings, I go by MIA MAYHEM.

I'm still really new at being super—that's why I go to the Program for In Training Superheroes, aka the PITS! The PITS is a top secret superhero-training academy. And thanks to the things I've learned, I've been able to save the day before school even starts!